D0320457

THE ADVENTURES OF Shirley HOLMES™

THE CASE OF THE

ALIEN ABDUCTIONS

Screenplay novelisation by
Sue Mongredien

Collins
An imprint of HarperCollinsPublishers

Published in Great Britain by Collins in 1998
Collins is an imprint of HarperCollins*Publishers*Ltd
77–85 Fulham Palace Road, Hammersmith,
London W6 8JB

1 3 5 7 9 8 6 4 2

Created by Winklemanis
Original screenplay by Elizabeth Stewart
Copyright © Shirley Holmes Productions 1998

ISBN 0 00 675370 1

Printed and bound in Great Britain by
Caledonian International Book Manufacturing Ltd,
Glasgow

THE LEGACY

To the holder of this letter, my commendations.

Solving the puzzle of the chest required more than considerable deductive powers...

My work has consumed my life and I have produced no heir to follow in my path. But I picture you – a young man of good imagination. Any mystery devised by mortal mind can be solved therewith...

Yours faithfully,
Sherlock Holmes

Shirley Holmes would never forget the day she first discovered the secret of the trunk. It had been in the attic for years and most of the time it lay half-forgotten, buried under the usual sort of clutter that no one uses but can't bear to throw away.

From time to time, Shirley would

remember its existence and go and take a look at it. The trunk was a mahogany chest and she enjoyed feeling its intricately carved surface, exploring the patterned grooves of the exotic flora and fauna depicted there. She always wondered what could possibly be inside such an imposing and fascinating receptacle. Her gran didn't know – couldn't even remember where the chest had come from, except that she thought her husband had inherited it from a relative.

The fact that the trunk was locked only roused Shirley's curiosity further, but nobody knew where the key was and it was far too beautiful to break into.

On Shirley's twelfth birthday, the trunk caught her eye again. This time her attention focused on the worn brass plate on the front. On it was etched a series of letters in the Cyrillic alphabet, followed by the numbers: 14551485. It looked like some sort of manufacturer's code, but today's examination of the scratched, metallic surface made Shirley's heart beat faster…

The first thing she noticed was that the letters weren't all Cyrillic – there were also some Arabic and Greek letters. At once Shirley set to work deciphering the letters, which revealed a simple sentence in English: 'Look for clue in 14551485'.

Shirley's mind raced. What could the numbers mean? She tried adding them, multiplying them, organising them in patterns… and then, suddenly, it became clear to her. Pulling down a history book from her shelves she flicked through the pages and a satisfied grin flickered over her face as she read aloud, "1455 to 1485. The

Wars of the Roses. *Yes!*"

But solving one puzzle had only led to another – a scenario that was to become very familiar to Shirley after that day. What on earth could the translation of the message on the brass plate possibly mean? She read the sentence aloud, to see if speaking the words helped in any way.

"Look for clue in the Wars of the Roses."

Furrowing her brow, the girl examined the trunk once more – and discovered an ornate carving of two entwined roses on one side. She ran her fingers along the design – and, suddenly, a latch flipped open. A secret compartment was revealed, inside which was a key…

Holding her breath, Shirley unlocked the chest and raised the heavy lid. She gazed at the contents – not gold or jewels, but it was a unique treasure all the same. Her sharp eyes took in the pile of old diaries and a few musty clothes, the battered violin and a little case containing a pair of gold-rimmed spectacles.

Then she gasped and picked up a deerstalker hat. At once she knew to whom the trunk had belonged – her great-great-uncle, the famous detective Sherlock Holmes.

Shirley knew all about her ancestor. She had apparently inherited his thirst for knowledge, his eye for detail and his ability to solve intricate problems. Somehow, finding her way into this horde of his most private possessions made Shirley feel a true affinity with the man. Instinctively, she also knew that there would be something in the chest that was meant for her.

Carefully rifling through the items,

she passed over ancient relics, glass bottles of foul-smelling liquids and strange, exotic weapons. Finally, tucked into a small shelf in the lid, she discovered the letter…

Avidly, Shirley read the message from beyond the grave. It was definitely written to her – even though Great-uncle Sherlock seemed to think she ought to be a boy.

But if the contents of the letter weren't exactly what she'd been hoping for, they made her determined of one thing: that she would prove a *niece* was just as capable of carrying forth Sherlock Holmes's legacy as a nephew!

Shirley Holmes, detective, was created that day and things were never, ever the same again…

The university bus station was deserted and quiet. The last bus had parked up well over an hour ago and was now locked away in the shed, its engine cold. The staff were long gone, too – back to their warm, cosy homes for the night. A tin can rattled in the gutter with a gust of wind, before falling silent once more.

A lone figure suddenly rounded the corner, making a bizarre sight in the dark, empty street. He was dressed in a pink pig costume – complete with floppy ears and a plastic snout – and carried a real black pig under his arm, which was grunting and trying to escape. The pig was wearing the university colours of maroon and gold around its neck and wasn't enjoying this midnight adventure at all.

"Shut up!" hissed the costumed man to his noisy companion. He hurried through the bus station and on to a wooded path, looking anxiously over his shoulder the whole time. The pig bucked once more and dug its trotters into the man's chest, squealing even louder.

"*Shut up!*" hissed the young man again, squeezing it tighter. He couldn't let the pig go now. He'd had his instructions. Without the pig, it could all go horribly wrong…

Without the street lights to guide him, it became harder to see as the path led deeper into the woods. Branches scraped at the man's face, tree roots caught at his feet and made him stumble, and he flinched nervously at every sound. The pig continued to squeal, scrabbling frantically to be let down as the unlikely pair went on and on, deeper into the undergrowth.

"Guys? I got him!" called the man at last. He stopped in a clearing, awaiting a reply. His hoarse voice sounded loud in the thick darkness and the pig grunted an echo, its legs still flailing.

Suddenly a dazzling light shone on the young man's face. He blinked into it, blinded by the glare.

"Guys?" he called again, a note of panic creeping into his voice. "Is that you? Guys, stop fooling around!"

There was still no answer and the man stood waiting, his heart pounding, his eyes desperately trying to scan through the beam to see where it was coming from. All at once the light shining on his face grew brighter and more intense, and a howling wind started up.

"Guys?" he called one last time, but his words were swallowed up in the roar of the wind. His pig snout blew off as the gale howled around him and the white light glared horribly bright. Then there was a sudden scream of terror... followed by silence.

CHAPTER 1

"Concentrate," Gran was saying. "Focus inside of you…"

It was a sunny morning at the Holmes's house and Gran was taking Shirley through some t'ai chi movements before breakfast. Gran was an expert in t'ai chi and was trying to teach Shirley a series of movements designed to improve balance and co-ordination. The pair of them stood in front of the kitchen counter, swaying in unison and practising the rhythmic hand movements. It was surprisingly complicated; after all, it was still first thing in the morning!

Although Shirley was trying her hardest to concentrate on the moves Gran was teaching her, it was pretty difficult trying to block out the buzz of her dad's business call right behind them. Dad was a diplomat at the Embassy and was in the middle of trying to organise some sort of peace talks – a conversation Shirley would normally have found interesting to listen in on. He had been working on the conference details for weeks and Shirley had thought the whole thing was just about tied up now. The phone call seemed to be taking for ever, though – it wasn't like Dad to make so much *fuss...*

"I'm happy to cooperate with the media, but security must come first..." he was saying firmly.

Shirley glanced over her shoulder, then frowned as she tried to ignore his words. It was hard work, having to close her ears to something deliberately when usually her detective instincts required her to eavesdrop and remember *everything* for future reference! You never knew *what* was going to turn out to be useful information, and Dad's line of work meant she could usually eavesdrop on some pretty fascinating conversations...

"Let your mind relax," urged Gran, glancing at Shirley's face, and Shirley made one last effort to forget about Dad as he snapped shut the briefcase and made to leave.

"The location must remain top

secret," he said behind her. "We'll hold a press conference the moment the peace talks have concluded, you have my word…"

Shirley continued the exercises, but her ears had automatically pricked up at the words 'top secret'. Hmmm, what was the big deal here, then? Why so hush-hush? Secrets were meant to be investigated, in Shirley's opinion!

"Let nothing distract you…" said Gran encouragingly over Mr Holmes's words.

But Shirley *was* distracted – not only by the phone call, but also at the sight of her dad halfway out of the door while his packed lunch was still on the kitchen counter.

"Dad – lunch!" she called, grabbing the bag of sandwiches and then turning round swiftly so that she blocked his path. She thrust the bag at him and he laughed.

"Thanks, sweetheart!" he said. "I'd forget my own head if it wasn't for you, sometimes!"

As he left the house, Shirley turned to her grandmother with a guilty expression on her face. "Sorry, Gran. Focal failure," she said.

Gran smiled and gave Shirley a hug. "That's enough for today, anyway. You're coming along very well," she said. "Now – let's have some breakfast! You've earned it!" She passed Shirley a banana and started peeling an orange for herself.

Shirley flipped on the TV set as she peeled the banana.

"And now for the local news," a reporter began, and Shirley blinked in surprise as a pig's snout suddenly grunted wetly on the screen. "Daisy the pig, mascot of the Redington Rockets football team, is credited with alerting passers-by to the latest victim in a series of unexplained assaults."

Shirley leant closer to the set with interest. A heroine pig? This *had* to be good! The camera cut to the Redington university campus, where a young female witness was explaining how the noisy squealing of the pig had led them to the latest victim in the university grounds.

"We heard it from the top of the woods," she said breathlessly. "Daisy was squealing like *crazy*! So a bunch of us rushed down to see what had happened to her – and there was this guy on the ground – out cold!"

There was then a shot of the victim dodging the news camera, his university sports jacket pulled up over his head as he ran into one of the colleges. Shirley read the name on his jacket with interest.

"The man, believed to be a Redington University student, refused to file a complaint," the reporter continued. "Police are baffled as to a motive behind the assaults, which so far have left three Redington residents unconscious but otherwise unharmed." She stopped and smiled out of the screen. "One victim, however, has this explanation," she finished.

A stocky construction worker appeared on the screen, his eyes wild as he spoke into the camera. 'MIKE HALSEY, VICTIM' the caption read.

"I'm telling you, it was aliens!" he said urgently. "There was this big light dazzling me so I couldn't see – then this wind whipped up from outta nowhere, and then… and then I don't remember a thing!"

Shirley's eyebrows rose, but before she could learn any more, the TV was abruptly switched off…

"Idiots!" exclaimed Gran.

Shirley jumped. "Who?" she asked. "The police?"

"The aliens!" said Gran indignantly. "Why bother with these silly abductions when thousands of people would give their right arms to go on their spaceships?" She sighed and smiled at her granddaughter. "They could sell *tickets*!"

Shirley bit into her banana thoughtfully. Aliens in Redington? Gran looked almost sorry *she* hadn't been the one abducted in the university woods.

Shirley wasn't sure what to make of the whole story… it all sounded most peculiar. Still, being Shirley Holmes, she wasn't about to leave the matter unresolved if she could help it. That just wasn't her style! And so, minutes later, as she packed her rucksack, she made sure to include her emergency mobile phone and a container of plaster of Paris, along with her lunch and school books. This looked like being the start of an interesting case and she would make sure she got right to the bottom of it – aliens, pigs and all!

CHAPTER 2

History was the first lesson of the day and Mr Howie was asking students to read out their homework essays to the rest of the class. For the second time that morning, Shirley found it impossible to concentrate. She wriggled in her chair restlessly and stared out of the window up into the blue sky outside. Just at this moment, history didn't hold as much interest for her as the thought of aliens. Besides, there was far too much going on in her mind for her to be able to pay much attention to school-work!

On the way to school, she'd made a quick detour through the university woods, on the look-out for clues. She thought she might as well get stuck into the case as soon as possible – especially before curious alien-spotters had the chance to trample away any precious evidence! And she felt quite smug that she'd thought to bring along the plaster of Paris – her hunch about finding some interesting footprints to make casts of had been absolutely right.

As she followed the path down through the woods, she wondered what exactly had happened the night before. It must have been so dark there she couldn't possibly hope to find any witnesses who would have noticed anything going on. The woods were always pretty remote at night. The aliens had obviously chosen their spot carefully...

Well, she would just have to check it out thoroughly herself. Aha! What was that?

Shirley crouched down and stared intently at the ground. The sneaker prints she had been following had stopped suddenly. This must have been where it all happened! She poured the gooey plaster of Paris into a particularly deep footprint and then spotted a set of four smaller prints nearby. They would belong to Daisy the pig. So, who else had been there?

Shirley carefully took casts of the two different footprint types and then looked around hopefully for something else to help with the puzzle. Then she gasped and stared at the ground only metres from where she was crouching. She couldn't quite believe what she was seeing…

"Shirley Holmes! Are you still with us?"

Mr Howie's voice jerked her back into the lesson and miles away from all thoughts of aliens. Shirley just about managed a nod.

"Good! Glad to hear it! Now then… Bart! I do believe it's your turn to read your essay." Mr Howie waved his hand and looked expectantly at Bart, one of his best students. At least he could count on Bart to always do his homework, even if sometimes it was a little… well… long-winded.

Bartholomew James III went up to the front of the classroom and cleared his throat. Shirley groaned inwardly.

Great. Sometimes Bart's long essays were enough to send you to sleep!

"Archaeologists believe that the Great Pyramid was built by slaves as a grand tomb for the Pharaoh," he began reading, and then paused dramatically. "But they are *wrong!*"

There was something about Bart's tone of voice that made Shirley look up at him as he continued. "The Great Pyramid was in fact built by beings from another galaxy, in other words… extraterrestrials!"

There were a few sniggers at this, but Mr Howie wasn't amused. He glared at Bart. "Is this your idea of a joke, Mr James?" he asked sternly. Mr Howie took assignments very seriously, unfortunately.

"No, sir!" protested Bart, sounding hurt. "I've done tons of research. The Egyptians even drew pictures of their Sun God flying around in a spacecraft…"

Almost the whole class was grinning. Boy, was Bart going to get ticked off for this! All eyes turned to Mr Howie to see how he was going to take Bart's extraordinary essay.

"Sit down, Bart," groaned Mr Howie wearily. "This is a history class, not a Star Trek convention!"

But Bart wasn't going anywhere. He was on a roll! "If you multiply the height of the pyramid by a thousand million, you get almost the exact distance between the Sun and the Earth!" he told the class earnestly.

"Sit *down*, Bart!" repeated Mr Howie, glaring and tapping his pen on the desk.

Bart looked sadly at his teacher. "Mr Howie, the truth is out there. It's nothing to be afraid of."

This was too much for Mr Howie, and his eyes narrowed at Bart. "Right!" he said coldly. "I warned you! Tomorrow morning, first thing, I want two thousand words from you – headed 'There's a Rational Explanation for Everything'!"

Shirley saw her friends Bo and Alicia look at each other, feeling sympathy for Bart. Ouch! Two thousand words was a bit steep! Unlucky!

Bart was about to argue, but thought better of it at the last minute and sat down. Thankfully the bell rang at that moment, before Mr Howie had a chance to hand out any more punishments. Shirley stared at Bart with new interest as she packed away her belongings. Perhaps he might be able to help with her new case...

It was a relief to get out of the classroom – Mr Howie really got mad at times and then it was best to stay out of his way.

"Phew!" sighed Bo as he left the classroom with Shirley and Alicia. "Time just goes *backwards* in that class, I swear it!"

"Maybe we were in some sort of *alien* timewarp," said Alicia with a wicked giggle as they passed Bart at his locker in the corridor.

"Yeah, good joke, man!" added Bo. "You got him going there!"

Bart gave them both a hard stare through his glasses. "Laugh all you want, but at least I'm psychologically prepared for the inevitable!" he said fiercely.

Bo and Alicia smirked at each other. Bart could be pretty far out at times – and this was obviously one of those times!

Shirley was more thoughtful. "Bart, what do you know about Close Encounters?" she asked him, curiously. After this morning's findings it looked like she was going to have to call in some expert advice.

Bart looked to see if Shirley was setting him up, then smiled, relieved to be taken seriously at last. "Why, what do you need to know?" he said. "I've got a whole bunch of magazines you can check out, if you're interested…"

"I am," said Shirley quickly. "We'll be round after school – right, Bo?"

"Er… right," said Bo in surprise. Then he looked at Shirley. "Uh-oh. Does this mean…?"

Shirley grinned back at him. She was never happier than when she had an unsolved mystery on her hands.

"Oh, yes!" she said. "It means we're in business!"

CHAPTER 3

Despite having teased Bart earlier, even Bo was taken-aback at the sight of Bart's lawn when he and Shirley went round later that afternoon. Bart obviously had been serious about everything he said, for the grass was cut into an elaborate pattern of circles… lots of circles!

"What the…?" said Bo in disbelief. He turned to Bart. "What *is* this? Some sort of self-portrait in grass?"

"It's a landing site," said Bart proudly, dumping a pile of magazines into Shirley's arms. "You know, like a crop circle. I copied it from pictures of the ones in England. It's for when they come back."

"For when *who* come back?" asked Bo suspiciously.

"The ETs!" answered Bart cheerfully. "Every couple of years, Redington turns into UFO Central. It's due to happen any time now, and this" – he pointed at the circles, then gazed wistfully up into the sky – "is my way of saying, 'Hey, pick me!'"

Bo stared at him. "You're saying you actually *want* to be abducted by aliens? You want them to pick you?"

"Sure!" Bart smiled. "Who wouldn't?"

Bo rolled his eyes at Shirley, unsure of how to reply, but Shirley didn't notice. She was deep in thought, engrossed in one of the magazines.

"What do they look like?" she said at last. "Any pictures in here? Or photographs, even?"

Bart flicked through one of the magazines importantly. "At least eight different species of alien have been documented so far," he informed them, "but these are the guys doing most of the abducting. This is an artist's impression."

He passed the magazine over to Shirley and she stared at it in fascination. There, in the centre pages, was a drawing of a small grey creature with a bulbous head. It had large, almond-shaped eyes with only a slit for its nose and mouth.

"Hey, it's Ms Stratmann!" joked Bo, referring to Sussex Academy's rather strict head teacher. He put on a Martian voice. "Take me to your homework!"

Shirley stared at the alien's blank expression for a second, and then over at the separate picture of its three-toed, reptilian feet. As she looked at the three long toes, she felt a shiver run down her spine.

She closed the magazine with a snap. "Come on, Bo! Let's go – we've got work to do!"

"We do?" replied Bo, but Shirley was already halfway down the path. "Never a dull moment," he sighed to Bart, and then, "Wait up!" he called, running after her.

Back at Shirley's attic bedroom, the girl opened her rucksack and began to empty out the contents. The place looked like a cross between a museum, an office and a laboratory. She had spent a long time getting it organised to her satisfaction and it was the base from which she studied every case she worked on.

Bo picked up a large stone from a shelf and started tossing it between his hands while he waited to hear what this was all about. Shirley had hardly said a word all the way home and now she was fiddling around with a shoe-box, unwrapping something in it.

"Don't tell me you dragged me all the way over here to see your new shoes," he said, trying to provoke her into revealing something of what she was thinking.

Shirley looked up briefly and pulled a face. "These are not shoes. Just wait," she said.

"So, you're telling me you actually

believe that there are little green guys running around Redington, snatching people?" said Bo dryly, still tossing the stone between his hands.

Shirley didn't look up from her box. "Little *grey* guys," she corrected. "And I'd be careful with that. Petrified mammoth dung is very rare, you know."

Bo stopped what he was doing immediately and put the dung gingerly back on the shelf, wiping his hands on his trousers afterwards. He stared at it, and then at Shirley. He knew she was weird, but sometimes he found her *totally* weird.

"That's nice to have around the house," he commented, and then, "So you *do* believe it," he pressed, as he watched Shirley closely.

Shirley shrugged. "I believe in keeping an open mind," she said.

"And certain areas are known to be alien hot-spots for sure – Mexico City, for example, and somewhere in Florida…"

"Yeah, but *Redington*?" said Bo in disbelief.

Shirley shrugged once more. "Why not? There were sixteen sightings in Redington in one month alone two years ago," she said.

"So they took a wrong turn at Alpha Centauri!" said Bo. "So what?"

Shirley gave him one of her looks, then passed him one of the plaster casts she'd unwrapped from the box. "So, what do you make of this?"

Bo stared at the imprint of a sneaker she was holding in front of his face. He ran his fingers over its ridges and considered.

"Size … 11? Road Sports brand,"

he said. "What of it?"

"And this?" Shirley passed him a second casting.

Bo pushed up his nose and grunted. "Pig's hoof," he said.

"Very convincing! Just like Daisy!"

Shirley paused dramatically. "Now… this one."

She passed Bo a third casting and stood expectantly, arms crossed.

Bo stared at it – and then at Shirley. The casting was of another footprint, but this one had three long, curved toes and looked suspiciously like the footprint of an… alien!

CHAPTER 4

The plaster cast footprint had completely convinced Bo that something unearthly had visited Redington and he was now as keen as Shirley to get to the bottom of the mysterious abductions. One phone call later and they were cycling to the university in search of further information.

"An alien footprint! I can't believe that was an alien footprint!" he kept saying excitedly. "A real live alien footprint!"

Shirley sighed in exasperation. "I said to keep an open mind, Bo," she said, trying to pedal out of hearing range.

As the pair of them rounded a corner and pulled up outside one of the university colleges, they stopped in surprise at the sight of a young man in a sports jacket hanging upside down from a pulley. He was pinching his nose between two fingers and breathing deeply and noisily, with a distinctive nasal whine. It sounded a bit weird, and both Shirley and Bo approached him with some care. So *this* was the guy who'd been found in the woods last night. Did that strange whine have anything to do with his experience? Was he now communicating in Martian?

Shirley glanced at his sneakers, and then at Bo. "Road Sports!" she whispered, pointing to them.

The upside-down guy's eyes jerked open at the sound of her whisper and he stared at the two visitors nervously. "Who are you?"

"I'm Shirley – he's Bo," said Shirley briskly. "I saw you on the news this morning – Alan."

Alan shot her a suspicious look. "How do you know my name?" he asked.

"I saw your jacket on TV," Shirley told him. "Then I phoned your college. They *said* I'd find you hanging around somewhere."

Alan scratched his neck awkwardly and Shirley leant in for a closer look. He seemed to have rather a sore spot there. Hmmm – could be evidence of alien probing. She'd read about something like this in Bart's magazines.

"Bunch of jerks!" he was moaning. "Like I asked to have that stupid news camera in my face! And so many of them, all hassling me about last night!" He paused for a second. "Hey, could you let me down?"

Bo moved forward, but Shirley stopped him before he could help.

"What happened last night?" she demanded. Might as well make the most of Alan's vulnerable position while she could!

Alan blinked in surprise at the question. "What are you – a baby cop?"

Not the answer Shirley had wanted! She pursed her lips at his reply and looked meaningfully at Bo, who immediately stepped forward and set Alan spinning on his pulley.

Alan was not into the spinning at all! "OK, OK!" he yelled. "I'll tell you! But get me down first – all the blood's rushing to my head!"

With another look from Shirley, Bo stopped Alan spinning and the pair of them eased him to the ground. He untied his feet and stood up shakily, holding his head as if it were about to come off. He ran a hand through his dark brown curls, and exhaled heavily.

"That's better," he said. "These relaxation exercises are good, but after a while they make you feel pretty dizzy."

"Well?" prompted Shirley, eager to get the details. "What happened to you?"

"OK, here's what happened," Alan began. Then he leant in towards them, lowering his voice. Shirley and

Bo both stared expectantly at Alan, dying to know more.

Alan cleared his throat, and then seemed to change his mind at the sight of their fascinated faces. Hey, he wasn't about to be turned into a freak show by a couple of kids!

"Nothing happened," he said finally. "It was just a joke. So why don't you two midgets get lost?!"

With that, he turned and began walking away – but not before Shirley had caught another glimpse of the red patch on his neck that he'd been scratching.

"What's that on your neck?" she called after him. "Alan?"

Alan ignored her, and revved up his motorbike with a roar. All these questions – he was getting out of there!

Bo grabbed Shirley's arm. "Shirley…" he started, but she wasn't listening.

"What's that on your neck?" she yelled again over the drone of the motorbike.

Alan drove away without an answer. Shirley watched him disappear with great frustration. She seemed to be getting nowhere fast today!

"Shirley," Bo repeated patiently, then pulled her round to face him. "It's a *hickey* – you know, from his girlfriend."

Shirley looked down, embarrassed for a second, but then frowned, thinking back to Bart's magazines. *Was* it a hickey? She wasn't so sure...

That night, Mr Howie left school later than usual. It had been a long day and he was looking forward to getting home. It was dark and rainy as he stepped into the school car park

– and then suddenly it became even darker still as the street light behind him flickered, buzzed weakly and died out.

Mr Howie shivered and looked quickly over both shoulders as he increased his pace and walked swiftly on to his car, shielded by an umbrella. For some reason he felt nervous of the dark tonight. It felt as if something was going to happen.

He fumbled with his key in the car door, then dropped it on the pavement. He wasn't sure why he had started feeling so nervous, but there was a sick feeling building in his stomach. He stooped down to find his car key… and as he did so, a gust of wind blew harshly against him, chilling his bare fingers as they scrabbled on the ground. The wind blew again, harder this time, turning the umbrella inside-out and almost out of his grasp. Where had that sudden squall come from? It had been so still all day.

Mr Howie suddenly became aware of a dazzling light right behind him. He rose slowly and turned, shielding his eyes from the glare of the light, as the trees tossed around him in the howling wind.

"No," he muttered in disbelief as he stared into the white light. A figure seemed to be emerging from the glare and was slowly coming towards him.

It was hard to see properly, but the figure appeared to be thin and grey all over, with a bulbous head and almond-shaped eyes...

"No!" he repeated, shaking his head as the strange creature approached. "Nooooooo!"

CHAPTER 5

"I gave birth to an alien baby!" Bo announced incredulously from where he was leaning under the tree outside school. "Aliens took my kidney! Man, that's gotta hurt!"

While Bo picked out the more sensational headlines from the UFO publication he was reading, Shirley practised Gran's t'ai chi movement once more. She still couldn't get it *quite* right – and it was pretty hard to concentrate with Bo jabbering away next to her. Ever since she'd shown him the three-toed cast, he'd been more and more fascinated by the supernatural. As far as he was concerned, Bart was right – Redington was about to turn into UFO Central. It was only a matter of time now before they were invaded by the little grey men in Bart's magazine!

Bo looked at Shirley pointedly. "They're newspaper *headlines*," he said. "From *The Blazing Comet*. Pay attention!"

Shirley looked at him sternly. "Remember what I said to you about keeping an open mind?" she said. "Nothing's certain yet. Until I see an alien with my own eyes, I'm not convinced – and neither should you be!"

Bo pulled a face. "You've seen its *footprints*! What more should it have done? Left you a note? Phoned for a chat about the problems of shoe-shopping when you've only got three toes?"

Before Shirley could reply, a figure stumbled past them along the path, clutching a brown paper bag and looking deep in thought. They almost didn't recognise him. His white hair, normally neatly brushed down, stood up wildly on end, as if he had been running his hands through it all morning.

Right behind him came a rather anxious-looking Bart.

"Mr *Howie*?" he called hesitantly. He had followed the teacher from the hall and was almost too nervous to approach him. He could hardly believe his eyes at how strange –

almost manic – Mr Howie looked today.

Mr Howie jumped a mile at the sound of his name.

"What?" he snapped, whirling round to face Bart. "Don't sneak up on people!"

Bo and Shirley both stared at the scene in curiosity – it wasn't like their history teacher to be quite so edgy. OK, he got mad sometimes, but he was never so... jumpy.

Bart meekly tried to hand Mr Howie several sheets of paper. The history teacher looked back at him blankly, as if he'd never seen the boy before, let alone knew why he was giving him anything.

"It's my essay," Bart reminded him. "You know – 'There's a Rational Explanation for Everything'. Remember?"

Mr Howie looked at the boy and seemed to calm down. "Yes," he muttered. "Yes, of course there is." Then he turned and walked away.

Bart walked off too, still clutching his essay. Shirley could read the thoughts on his face as clearly as if he had spoken them aloud – adults were just so inconsistent at times!

Typically, Bo was the first to comment.

"Howie looks like he spent the night partying," he remarked to Shirley.

"I wonder what's in the bag," was all she said, staring after their teacher, who was rubbing his neck feverishly as he disappeared into the school building.

Little did Shirley know that the bag in fact contained a copy of the same trashy newspaper that Bo had been reading – although, unlike Bo, Mr Howie had hardly dared to look at it. It was only once he was safely in the classroom with the door firmly shut that he took *The Blazing Comet* out of its wrapping, reading the alien headlines with a shudder. Now, where was that picture he'd been looking at in the shop...?

Then the sound of his name made the teacher jump once more.

"Mr Howie? Urgent telephone call for you in the school office!" came the message over the school intercom system.

Sighing with frustration, Mr Howie hid the newspaper under a stack of essays and left the room.

Shirley and Bo watched as their teacher rushed down the corridor, then grinned at each other. Shirley shut her mobile phone and nodded to Bo to keep guard in the corridor as she slipped into the empty classroom. Now, where was that paper bag Mr Howie had been carrying? Ah, there it was – but it was empty!

She rifled through the files on his desk until she found... *The Blazing Comet* – full of the same gory alien stories that Bo had been enjoying. So *this* was what her teacher had been clutching so urgently! Very interesting! But why? Especially after Bart's little lecture yesterday...

Before she could discover any more, she heard Bo's loud, "Hi, Mr Howie! How are you?" from outside in the corridor.

Uh-oh – the warning signal.

When Mr Howie had reached the school office, it had totally freaked him out to discover that there was no one at the other end of the phone. Was someone playing tricks on him? he wondered as he rushed straight back to the classroom.

He eyed Bo sternly when the boy spoke. "Perfectly fine, thank you," he replied gruffly. "Why shouldn't I be?"

Mr Howie came back into the classroom before the conversation could go on any longer, shutting the door behind him. Shirley leapt into a cupboard to hide – just in time!

The cupboard was dark and musty, and Shirley crouched on a pile of text-books, praying they wouldn't topple over and give her hiding place away. She certainly didn't want to be caught spying – but she was also sure that if the teacher discovered her there he'd go to pieces completely!

She opened the door a crack to watch as Mr Howie sat down at his desk, uncovered the newspaper once more and resumed his reading. She sat very still, able to feel his tension in the air. She knew that the slightest noise would make him jump instantly. What *was* wrong with him?

As he turned a page, Shirley saw the teacher's eyes widen with fear and the newspaper shook between his trembling fingers. His breath started to come loudly and nervously through his nostrils as he read the rest of the article. He pinched his nose and breathed even louder, until it almost sounded like an animal's whine, Shirley thought to herself.

Wait a minute... where had she

heard that exact same nasal breathing the day before? Of course – Alan Brooks had done it, when he'd been hanging upside down from the pulley. Strange! Relaxation exercises, he'd said at the time. But how come Mr Howie was doing it too?

Shirley looked over at her teacher again, and her own eyes widened in surprise. What was that on Mr Howie's *neck*?

Shirley gulped. There was a big red welt on her teacher's neck that definitely hadn't been there the day before. Definitely! A top sleuth like herself would have spotted some thing like that long ago.

She thought hard, trying to put together all this strange information as she sat motionless in the cupboard. Alien stories in the newspaper… a strange kind of nasal breathing… red welts appearing on people's necks… There was definitely *something* very strange going on in Redington. The question was – what?

... ... up. Shirley ...

CHAPTER 6

As Shirley updated him on her latest discovery, Bo wasn't so sure that their crusty old teacher could possibly be involved in anything as exciting as aliens. It just didn't fit.

"C'mon," he reasoned, "who would want to abduct *Howie*? And why? I bet they got rid of him pretty quickly once they'd realised their mistake!"

"Well, who would want to give

him a hickey?" countered Shirley. "And in the exact same spot as Alan's!" Suddenly she stopped dead in her tracks. "Bart!" she exclaimed, striding off purposefully.

Bo froze at this bizarre thought. "Mr Howie and *Bart*?" he called in amazement. "Are you serious?"

Shirley ignored him, and caught up with Bart who was at the bicycle shed. "Bart, what do you know about alien 'implants'?" she asked urgently.

"They're tracking devices," Bart told her, pushing up his glasses. "They usually look like tiny ball-bearings. Often found up the abductee's nose. Sometimes in the neck."

Bo joined them and found himself rubbing his nose uncomfortably at Bart's remarks. Didn't seem to be any ball-bearings in there! But in the neck... would you be able to feel a ball-bearing in your own neck?

Shirley tried to gather her thoughts. "So... if an abductee has one, does that mean the aliens are coming back for him?" she asked slowly.

Bart considered it. "Possibly," he replied. "There've been reports of double, even triple-abductees." He pulled a face in disgust. "Some people have all the luck!"

Shirley turned to Bo. "What kind of car does Mr Howie drive?"

"Er... it's that one over there," he told her, pointing across the car park. "The pale blue one, I think."

"Great," she said. "See you later!"

When Mr Howie left school that day, he wasn't taking any chances after what had happened in the car park the night before. Even though it was still broad daylight, he clutched an iron bar in one hand and looked wildly over his shoulder every few seconds. He went over to his car and opened the back door, tossing his briefcase on to the back seat.

Next second, he leapt back in alarm, as there came a muffled "ow!" from where his case had bounced off the seat on to a blanket on the floor. Mr Howie clutched the iron bar even tighter, as he pulled back the blanket, only to reveal...

"Miss Holmes!" Mr Howie didn't know whether to be angry or relieved to find that it was only Shirley in the back of his car. "What on earth do you think you're doing in here?"

Shirley tried a smile, although she didn't much like the look of the iron bar her teacher was waving in the air.

"It just seemed more efficient than trying to follow you on my bike..." she said weakly.

"*Follow* me?" roared Mr Howie.

Uh-oh. Shirley decided to cut to the quick. *She* certainly didn't want to be assigned any two-thousand word essays. "Just answer me one question," she said. "What happened to you last night?"

Mr Howie's eyes goggled as he struggled to keep his cool.

"I don't know what you're talking about!" he said tightly. "Now get out of my car!"

"But Mr Howie..." pleaded Shirley, but it was no good. The subject was *not* up for discussion.

"Get *out*!"

Mr Howie's pale blue eyes were coldly insistent and Shirley realised that there was nothing for it but to obey – although it was with great reluctance that she finally got out of the car. She stood and sighed as she watched her teacher drive away. Well, *that* plan had failed.

Bo, who'd seen the whole thing, joined Shirley once more.

"It seems I underestimated his paranoia," Shirley told him, folding her arms across her chest. She would just have to find some other way of getting information…

That evening Shirley hunched over her computer, scrolling through old newspaper articles in the search for more clues.

"No… no… no…" she muttered under her breath, skimming through story after story. Then she found an interesting-looking article that made her stop. 'MORE UFOS SIGHTED' read the headline, and she skimmed through the editorial eagerly. Perhaps this was what she had been looking for...

As she scrolled the text down further, a photo of Alan Brooks appeared on her screen. Shirley's eyes widened fractionally, and then out came one satisfied word as she finished reading the article: "Gotcha!"

Meanwhile, back at Sussex Academy, Ms Stratmann, the head teacher, sat working in her office. Leaning over the desk, she struggled to make the budget figures work for the next school year, grateful for the peace and quiet which was only to be found in the building at night.

But in another part of the building, someone else was busy, too: a silent figure pushed through the swing doors and went padding through the shadows of the dark hallway. On and on the figure walked, with slow, measured steps along the corridor, up to a locked door, where it stopped…

SMASH!

The noise of breaking glass could be heard all over the science block. Ms Stratmann jumped. What was that? She had thought she was the only member of staff left in the building! Was someone trying to break in to one of the laboratories?

She peered out of the office. Further down the dark corridor she could hear the clinking of glass bottles. Walking hesitantly, she crept closer towards the clinking, following the sound until she knew exactly which room it was coming from. There was definitely someone in there – and it didn't sound as if they had come along for extra studies!

Holding her breath, she peeped around the doorway and into the classroom. As a head teacher, Ms Stratmann had seen an awful lot of odd goings-on in the school – but she'd never been quite as surprised as this! There in front of her was a most unlikely-looking criminal: a man in *pyjamas* removing bottles of chemicals from one of the laboratory cabinets!

Ms Stratmann gasped, unable to help herself, and the man froze at the noise. He slowly turned around towards her, a glazed and far-away look in his eyes. The head teacher put her hand up to her mouth and her eyes went huge as she realised just who it was staring back at her.

"Mr *Howie*?" she exclaimed.

CHAPTER 7

The next morning, Shirley's dad gave
her a lift into school. The Embassy
peace conference was taking place
soon and security arrangements
really seemed to be hotting up,
judging from the black security
service car that tailed the limousine
all the way to Sussex Academy.

Shirley couldn't help squirming
uncomfortably on the smooth leather
upholstery, glancing out of the back
window at the black shadow purring

along behind them.

"Is all this really necessary?" she asked, uneasily. "There's not going to be any trouble, is there?"

Dad raised his eyebrows at her. "Peace conferences can be dangerous," he said, only half-joking. But another look at his daughter's face made him realise how worried it was making her feel. "It's quite normal, sweetheart," he reassured her. "All standard procedure."

"If you're sure…" Shirley said, doubtfully. She didn't like the thought of Dad having to be followed by security men. What did they think was going to happen to him that was so dangerous, anyway?

He smiled at her. "I'm sure," he said.

Nevertheless, when Shirley got out of the car to go to school, she found herself giving her dad a fierce hug. Sometimes she wished he would do something a bit safer than international diplomacy – even if it *did* mean limousine rides to school now and again. There was enough to keep her busy in her own life, without having to worry about Dad as well!

She walked along the hallway towards her form room. As she went past the science block, she saw to her surprise that Alicia was sweeping up broken glass in one of the laboratories.

Alicia paused in her sweeping and pulled a face at her friend. "Of course this had to happen while *I'm* science monitor!" she complained, leaning against the doorway. "Typical!"

"What happened?" asked Shirley, quickly.

"Howie went nuts," said Alicia conspiratorially. She looked around to check no one was listening before continuing. "He broke in here last night. In his *pyjamas*! Tried to steal some of the equipment – chemicals, I guess. There's broken glass everywhere, so I reckon he must have dropped a bottle or two when Stratmann sprung him. I'll probably go radioactive from this, knowing my luck."

She stiffened suddenly, and Shirley followed her gaze down the corridor, only to see Mr Howie himself, following Ms Stratmann into the head's office.

Alicia whistled at the sight. "Oh, man," she said, shaking her head. "He's in trouble now! Stratmann won't be happy about *that*!" Alicia looked rather happy, to be honest –

she loved nothing better than a good bit of real-life drama and was looking forward to being able to tell the rest of the class all about it. After all, she'd actually been on the scene of the crime this time!

Shirley nodded in agreement as she watched the office door swing shut behind them. Now, this was one conversation she would be *very* interested to hear…! How on earth was Mr Howie going to explain himself? – and more to the point, why on earth had he broken into the school?

Thinking quickly, she reached into her rucksack and got out a capsule of fake blood. Smearing a convincing amount of gore over her knee, she ran into the office after the teachers.

"My bicycle chain broke," she garbled to Mrs Fish, the school secretary, pointing at her knee.

Mrs Fish barely looked up from her typing. "Again?" she asked, pointedly.

Uh-oh… maybe it was time she thought of a new excuse, Shirley thought to herself. "Afraid so," she said. "My dad's supposed to be fixing it for me, but you know what *men* are like…" She shrugged, and crossed her fingers, willing Mrs Fish to feel the same way.

Luckily, *Mr* Fish was rather bad at getting round to fixing things in their household. Mrs Fish merely waved Shirley towards the nurse's room.

Excellent! Now for some prime eavesdropping! She mopped up the fake blood with a tissue and pressed herself against Ms Stratmann's door, listening intently.

"I don't know what to say," Mr

Howie was saying mournfully. "I don't remember a thing."

Poor Mr Howie! Shirley had been called into Ms Stratmann's office herself a few times and she knew just how intimidating it could be in there. Portraits of former head teachers glaring sternly down at you, the uncomfortable chair that made you squirm, the loud tick of the clock... She shuddered. Unlucky for some!

Shirley heard Ms Stratmann sigh. "Arthur," she said seriously, "you've taught here in good standing for thirty years. I don't want to file a report, but..."

"Oh, please," broke in Mr Howie. He sounded desperate. "Please don't do that!"

There was a pause and then Ms Stratmann said, in a kinder voice, "Maybe you need a break."

"No, I'm fine, really," Mr Howie began protesting, but Ms Stratmann interrupted firmly.

"I think it would be a good idea," she said, in a voice that wasn't to be argued with. Another pause and then, so low Shirley could hardly hear it, "Are you still seeing that psychiatrist?"

Shirley had to strain to catch Mr Howie's muttered response, and pressed her ear flat against the door. "I'm not crazy," was all he said.

Shirley leant back, trying to take everything in. But before she could work out how this new information fitted in with the alien abduction case – if it did at all – she heard footsteps approaching the door from the other side. She quickly dodged back out of sight, then peered around the corner to watch as Mr Howie left Ms

Stratmann's office.

Something about the way he carried himself – head down, shoulders slumped – made Shirley bite her lip in sympathy. He looked utterly miserable.

"Don't worry, Mr H," she said to herself. "I'll get to the bottom of this…"

She folded her arms across her chest. She *would* find out; she had to! So where now? Shirley tried to work out which was the best direction to take next.

The red welts, the breathing, now an attempted robbery and a psychiatrist. How did it all fit together? Or *did* it all fit together?

Whatever, she ought to get away from Ms Stratmann's office before she was found hanging around. Great detectives never got caught, after all!

She decided to try the school archive room to see if anything she could find there would help. There had to be an explanation behind the peculiar goings-on, there just had to be!

A little later, while she was scrolling through more news articles on the computer, she heard slow, heavy footsteps approaching. A bright light suddenly hit her from out of the gloom. Even from behind, the glare was dazzlingly intense.

Shirley wasn't easily fooled though, and without so much as a flinch, she smiled and said, simply, "Hi, Bo."

Bo turned the torch on his own face and frowned in disappointment. Shirley was impossible to scare!

"What are you doing down here?" he asked, rubbing his nose. Since Bart had told them about the alien implants, he'd found himself checking it – and his neck – at regular intervals. No alien was going to plant anything in *him*!

"Looking for a connection between Mr Howie and the other abductees," Shirley replied, busily tapping another name into the computer.

"You mean Mr Howie and that Alan guy?" asked Bo, leaning over her shoulder in interest.

"Mmm, *and* a construction worker," said Shirley.

A new article appeared on the screen, with a headline that read, 'BREAK-IN AT DEMOLITION SITE' and Shirley pointed to it.

"Look – the night after the construction worker was found unconscious, there was a break-in at the demolition site where he was working. *Detonators* were stolen."

Bo frowned, unable to make the connection. "So?"

Shirley stared at him. "Bo, last night, Mr Howie broke into where *he* works and tried to steal some ammonium hydroxide."

Bo considered this for a moment or two. "So the aliens are trying to make a bomb?" he joked. "What did Alan steal? Some college books, telling them how to build it?"

Shirley *wasn't* joking, though. "He hasn't stolen anything – yet," she said, seriously. "But I think you were right about the first bit. I think someone – or something – is using the abductees to steal components for a bomb, yes."

Bo's eyebrows shot up at her response. Alienbusting was one

thing, but talk of bombs was quite another.

"Whoa…" he said softly. "Shirley, I was only kidding…"

"I wasn't," said Shirley. "Mr Howie's connected to the construction worker by the robberies, and also to the college student by the implants." She looked at Bo. "And last night I found something out about Alan. This isn't the first time he's been abducted."

Bo whistled. "So, what next?" he said.

"What do you say we pay Alan another visit?" said Shirley. "Like now?!"

CHAPTER 8

It was a short cycle ride to the university. Once they were there, it didn't take long for Shirley and Bo to track down exactly where Alan lived in the hall of residence.

His room was one on a long corridor of student rooms. There was a photo on the outside of his door… a photo of Alan, which had been pierced through with several darts.

Although Shirley and Bo were

more than keen to see Alan and finally get some information out of him, it had to be said that Alan was distinctly unimpressed to see *them*. As he opened the door to see Shirley reading aloud from a newspaper, his heart sank into his boots. Not those kids again! Now what?

"'Missing teen found in corn field'," Shirley was saying with a pointed look. She folded up the newspaper and stared at him questioningly. "You told the police it was aliens, Alan. That you were abducted. What's the story?"

"The story is – get lost," growled Alan, trying to close the door in her face. Bo was too quick for him and stopped the door with his foot.

Shirley carried on as if nothing had happened. "That implant in your neck," she said sternly, nodding towards it meaningfully. "You know they'll be back."

Alan stared at her in disbelief and nervously touched the red patch on his neck.

"And not just once," said Bo in a hushed, hollow-sounding voice. He pulled out one of the darts from Alan's door, then stabbed it meaningfully into the photo. He stared into Alan's eyes. "Again... and again... and again," he said.

The scare tactics seemed to be working.

"Oh, man," Alan moaned, his face going slack. "My old man went into debt to pay for a shrink..." He seemed to be talking more to himself than Shirley and Bo, and they glanced at each other with interest.

"She finally convinced me it never happened," he muttered, staring at the floor. "Then it happens again…"

Shirley looked at the young man with new eyes, thinking quickly. An idea had just come to her.

"Your psychiatrist… would that be the specialist I read about?" She frowned and clicked her fingers, pretending she was trying to remember the name. "Doctor…"

Alan nodded glumly. "Yeah, Doctor Stavko," he said. He emerged from his room, locking the door behind him. Then his mood suddenly switched from mournful to brisk and he glared at the two intruders. "Look, I gotta go to work," he said. "And for the last time – leave me alone!"

Fat chance of *that*! As he headed off down the hall, Shirley waited a second, then whispered, "Follow him, Bo."

"Why?" Bo asked. Sometimes Shirley could be a bit bossy for his liking.

Shirley looked mysterious. "Because," she said vaguely, "they're not finished with him yet. And neither are we!"

Leaving Bo hot on Alan's trail, Shirley hurried back to school in search of Mr Howie. She found him in his classroom, packing away his belongings. As soon as he saw her, he put down a rolled-up map and pointed to the door.

"Out, Miss Holmes," was all he said.

"I know what happened to you," Shirley burst out, walking slowly up to his desk, eyes on his all the while. "You broke in here last night because you were told to. Post-hypnotic suggestion... messages fed to you through that implant!"

She pointed to the welt on his neck and Mr Howie's hand unwittingly flew up to touch it.

"Implant?" He gave her a hard stare.

"That thing in your neck," she explained. "It must be some kind of receiver. You've been getting hypnotic commands through it."

Mr Howie wasn't sure what to make of this news.

"Heavens, Miss Holmes, you're beginning to sound like Bart," he blustered, looking away from Shirley and carrying on with his packing.

Shirley put her hands on her hips. "It's up to you," she said, simply. "Either you believe me... or you believe that you're crazy."

Not much of a choice! Mr Howie

looked as if he didn't know which was worse. He blinked rather helplessly, and then turned to Shirley.

"What would you suggest?" he said, meekly.

Shirley held up a first-aid kit as her answer.

"May I please see your neck?" she asked.

CHAPTER 9

A little while later, with the help of a pair of tweezers, Shirley had removed a ball-bearing from her teacher's neck. She studied it under a magnifying glass as he looked on, horrified at this new turn of events.

"It's alien, isn't it?" he said in alarm. "I *was* abducted!"

Mr Howie pinched his nose tightly and started breathing heavily, with the same nasal whine as before. Shirley looked up at the sound, suddenly aware that she was on the verge of making the connection she'd been looking for all along.

"You're half right," she said. "You *were* abducted, Mr Howie. But not by aliens..."

She handed him the magnifying glass to see for himself and he peered through it at the ball-bearing in her hand.

"Made in Taiwan?" he read, puzzled. "But..."

Shirley didn't have time to explain – and she still wasn't entirely sure how the pieces of the puzzle fitted together, but she was starting to get an idea.

"Mr Howie, I need the name of your psychiatrist," she said firmly.

"What psychiatrist?" blustered Mr Howie uncomfortably. He avoided her eye and stared down at the magnifying glass again. Did this weird girl know *all* his secrets?

"I know you've been in therapy," Shirley replied in a matter-of-fact voice, "and I'm willing to bet it involves hypnotism." She looked closely at her teacher. "Is it Dr Stavko?" she asked, watching carefully for a reaction.

Mr Howie nodded – too surprised to cover up any longer. "Mirabella Stavko," he said. "How did you know?"

"Your breathing exercises," Shirley said dryly. "They're unique, to say the least!"

"It's a relaxation technique," Mr Howie explained. "Part of my therapy for kinderphobia."

"Kinderphobia?" echoed Shirley, leaning forward with interest.

Mr Howie looked at the floor,

embarrassed, and wished he hadn't mentioned it. "Fear of... er... children," he admitted.

At that moment Shirley's mobile phone rang and Mr Howie looked relieved at the interruption. He stared once more at the ball-bearing and touched his neck gingerly as Shirley fumbled in her bag for the phone.

"Bo?" she said, opening it up and holding it to her ear. "Any news?"

"Definitely," said Bo, sounding serious for once. "I followed Alan like you said. Something very weird is going on..."

"Where are you now?" Shirley asked him urgently.

"Outside the Redington Hotel," he answered. "Round the back. In the bushes, actually."

"Give me five minutes," said

Shirley. "I'm on my way!"

Four minutes later, Shirley had joined her co-sleuth and the two of them were sitting behind a good-sized bush, keeping an eye on the goings-on in front of them with the help of binoculars. They were watching the service entrance intently – and there was a lot to watch. Luckily, the hotel was surrounded by plenty of greenery, so they had a good vantage point.

The hotel was very busy, with lots of smart men and women in suits and sunglasses bustling around, looking important. A group of men in dark uniforms and sunglasses were making security checks and speaking urgently to each other on mobile phones. A big man in uniform was on the door of the service entrance, checking the name of every person going in or out on his clipboard. Whatever was going on was obviously big news.

Shirley whispered her findings from Mr Howie to Bo, and he listened intently. "Hypnosis?" he said finally. "As in, 'You are getting ve-e-ery sleepy'?"

Shirley nodded. "It doesn't work on everybody," she explained. "But a good hypnotist can tell if someone's suggestible almost at once, even by the way they flutter their eyelids."

Making sure Bo was looking straight at her, Shirley deliberately gave a fake yawn. Before he realised it, Bo found himself yawning too and Shirley giggled at the ease with which she'd tricked him. He frowned at her and turned his eyes back to the hotel. Sometimes Shirley Holmes was just too smart for her own good!

Then he noticed something of interest, and suddenly nodded towards the service entrance. "There's Alan," he said. "Turns out he works for a catering company."

They both watched Alan carefully for signs of hypnosis. Sure enough, he appeared to be in some kind of trance – he bumped into someone and didn't even notice. Then they watched him cross to the back of an open delivery truck and take out a large flower arrangement. He carried the flowers towards the service entrance, still with the same slow, trance-like walk.

"Man, he looks like a zombie!" commented Bo. "Reckon he's had a visit to Doctor Stavko?"

Shirley nodded in agreement. "Yes," she said, slowly. "But the question is, why? Why has she hypnotised him and sent him here?"

Bo surveyed the rest of the scene with his binoculars, searching for clues, then suddenly clutched Shirley's arm. "Hey – isn't that your dad?" he hissed.

Shirley glanced at him with alarm, before swinging her binoculars round to see. Sure enough, there was Dad, getting out of the limousine that had just pulled up. He stood talking with another official and then they both strolled into the building, right behind Alan and the flowers.

Something clicked in Shirley's mind. "It's the peace talks!" she gasped in horror, her mouth dropping open as she watched him.

"Oh my gosh! Bo – something terrible is going to happen! I have to warn Dad – and fast!"

CHAPTER 10

Bo thought quickly. "Have you got a pen and some paper?" he asked.

Shirley produced them without asking why and watched as Bo strode up to the big security guard on the door.

"Hi," said Bo, breathlessly. "Listen, it's true, isn't it? Madonna's staying here... You're her body-guard, right?"

The security guard was looking at his watch, and didn't seem to be paying attention. He obviously had better things to think about than children!

Shirley, realising what Bo was up to, took the opportunity to creep behind them towards the door, completely unnoticed.

"Who?" asked the agent, consulting the list of names he had on a clipboard.

"Madonna!" repeated Bo. "Do you think you could you get me her autograph?"

Shirley just had time to hear the agent asking which delegation Madonna was with, before slipping quietly inside the hotel. Any other time she would have chuckled at the guard's dumb answer, but right now she had more urgent things on her mind… like making sure her dad – and everyone else at the peace conference – was going to be safe.

She followed Alan and the flowers along a corridor, dodging behind a cart, a pile of boxes and various pillars along the way. What was he up to with those flowers?

Alan finally went into a reception room, put the flowers on a small table near the door and left again, still with the same zombie walk. Shirley was torn whether to follow him, or check out the flowers. She consulted her instincts which told her... go for the flowers!

As soon as he'd gone round the corner, Shirley snuck over to the bouquet to see if there was anything suspicious about it. She couldn't help thinking back to the dangerous items that had been stolen by the so-called abductees, and the conversation she and Bo had had about their reasons for it. "So the aliens are making a bomb?" Bo had joked. Shirley shivered at the memory of his words.

She pulled back the flowers to reveal... two wires and a detonator. She blinked as she realised she was looking straight at a small explosive device. So Bo had been right! Somebody *had* been making a bomb!

Shirley fought to stay calm. She had to act fast or the peace conference would become one major disaster.

Shirley fumbled in her rucksack and found a small pair of clippers. Holding her breath and using all her powers of concentration, Shirley reached for one of the wires leading out of the detonator... and then jumped as a hand gripped a tight hold of her wrist.

"That would be very foolish,"

came a cold voice. Shirley looked at the hand, at the expensive-looking gold bracelets around it, and then all the way up the arm, into the face of a petite, fifty-something woman who was standing next to her, glaring.

"Dr Stavko," said Shirley faintly, startled by her appearance. She hadn't heard the woman approaching, but now that she was standing in front of her, Shirley felt nothing but immense danger.

Dr Stavko smiled grimly. "You know who I am," she said, staring into Shirley's eyes. Her gaze was compelling.

"Even without your alien costume," retorted Shirley. At last, all the pieces of the puzzle had fallen into place. This was the woman behind all the strange goings-on – the 'alien' that Mr Howie had seen that dark night! And this woman wanted to blow up the peace conference – including her dad!

Dr Stavko gave Shirley a hard stare. An interfering child was quite the last thing she needed right now! "Clever girl," she said smoothly, disguising her annoyance. She watched with interest as Shirley's eyelids fluttered slightly.

Shirley blinked again, as though tired, and Dr Stavko decided to try out another plan. "It's warm in here, don't you think?" she said sympathetically, keeping her eyes locked on to Shirley's all the while.

Shirley flushed and loosened her collar slightly. It *was* warm; Dr Stavko was right. But she fought against the sudden sleepiness that overwhelmed her. "You got the idea from what Alan told you about being abducted before, didn't you?" she challenged, glaring at the doctor.

"His hallucinations were most vivid," Dr Stavko said, coldly.

"Your patients *trusted* you," Shirley said, accusingly.

Dr Stavko smiled the same grim smile once more. "There are people who have trusted me much longer," she said, an edge of pride creeping into her voice. "My people – in the resistance."

Shirley blinked again, her eyelids feeling heavy. The room seemed to be getting warmer every minute. "Why do you want to blow up your own peace conference?" she asked finally.

Dr Stavko stared into Shirley's eyes for a second more, before replying in a soothing kind of voice, "*Peace* without justice is not *peace*. Still, we all want *peace*..."

She stepped closer to Shirley, still holding her gaze mesmerisingly. Her voice became slower and heavier. "*Peace* and *serenity*," she continued. "That's all anyone wants…"

Shirley's eyelids blinked together at that moment, and stayed tightly closed. Dr Stavko smiled triumphantly. Easy! Then she pulled a remote control device out of her pocket and fiddled with the timer.

"Tranquility… calm…" she repeated slowly and soothingly, before pressing a button on the remote.

01:00, the timer read. 00:59, 00:58…

As the timer began ticking down the seconds, Dr Stavko carefully pushed the detonator back into the flower arrangement and handed the whole thing to Shirley.

"Perhaps you would be kind enough

to deliver these," she said firmly.

Shirley gazed back at her, eyes accepting and obedient.

CHAPTER 11

Still concealed in the bushes outside the hotel, Bo could see clearly through the double-glazed windows of the room where the delegates for the peace conference were gathering. Horrified, he watched Shirley gliding trance-like across the room with the flower arrangement in her hands. What was going on?

Although he hadn't seen the exchange with Dr Stavko, he knew instinctively that Shirley was in great danger.

Bo shook his head in bewilderment. Shirley – a zombie! It was unthinkable. And worse, he didn't have a clue how to help her.

Time ticked by, slowly but surely – 00:14… 00:13… 00:12… Bo didn't know it, but in another twelve seconds the whole hotel would blow up!

Shirley carried the flower arrangement in amongst the delegates. There were lots of official-looking men and women in smart suits – including her father – as well as several waiters and waitresses, loaded down with trays of drinks and snacks. From the looks of it, delegates had flown in from all over the world for the conference. Mr Holmes had certainly spent a long enough time working on all the organisational side of it.

Shirley stared straight ahead of her, eyes glassy and unseeing, as she walked across the room.

Dr Stavko stood near the exit, watching her. Excellent! Her plan was working perfectly. She glanced down at the remote-control timer she wore on her wrist to see that she had only ten seconds left to get out of there. Ten more seconds, and... BOOM!

Time to get moving! She started to edge discreetly out of the room, but a voice stopped her in her tracks.

"Dr Stavko!"

A delegate moved forward to shake her hand as she was backing away and Dr Stavko had a moment of panic. She had to get out there, make some excuse, before...

"Ambassador, how are you?" she

said quickly, giving him a sickly smile. She took another quick step back, her face turning pale, her smile becoming more and more fixed. "Ah, you'll have to excuse me, I've forgotten my notes…"

She backed away further, desperate to leave before any more precious seconds ticked away – but someone was blocking her path.

Shirley!

Shirley stared at the doctor with a vacant expression on her face before thrusting the flowers into her hands.

"For you, doctor," she said politely. Was that just a faint smile on her face?

It was Dr Stavko's worst nightmare. Just when everything seemed to be going right…! Her eyes widened with fear and she let out a blood-curdling scream as she threw the flowers into the air, as far away from her as possible.

"It's a bomb!" she yelled, cringing in terror as she waited for the blast. "It's the bomb!"

Then she clapped her hands over her ears, expecting the massive explosion any second. It had all gone so terribly wrong!

Everyone in the room jumped in horror as the high-pitched scream reached them all, and froze rigid. They all stared at Dr Stavko, and then stared down at the flowers. Then...

Nothing happened. Absolutely nothing. There was a moment's silence, broken only by Dr Stavko's nervous laugh as she tried frantically to work out what had happened, before Shirley leant in towards her, eyes narrowed in anger.

"My *father*'s in this room," she

said accusingly.

Security agents suddenly appeared and closed in on Dr Stavko. An alarm began to wail from the corridor and Shirley decided it was a good time to get out of there – especially as she'd just spotted her dad heading in their direction.

She slipped out of the room before he had a chance to see her, and went in search of Bo.

She found him just about to barge in through the now unguarded service door.

"Shirley! Thank goodness you're all right! I thought you were…"

Shirley smiled weakly and tapped her nose. "All in a day's work, Bo!" she said. Although she could do without *that* kind of work happening ever again!

As well as being hugely relieved to

see her, Bo had been most impressed with her performance, having watched the whole thing through the window. He gave her a huge clap on the back in delight when he heard the full details.

"So you made her think she hypnotised you, and you managed to cut the wires before the bomb had time to detonate," he said in admiration, trying to get the amazing story straight. "Shirley – that really looked a close one from where I was standing!"

Shirley nodded and smiled secretively. "Let's just say, I think Gran's t'ai chi lessons finally paid off."

Bo looked at her. "And now in English?" he prompted.

"My mind *was* being controlled," Shirley explained. "By me!"

CHAPTER 12

Talk about a long day! Shirley was relieved to get back home once it was all over. She decided to treat herself that night to a mega-snack. She'd earned it after all, she reckoned!

Humming happily to herself, she put together a ham, cheese and pickle tortilla, with various squirts of ketchup, mayonnaise and mustard. Yum! The perfect combination.

Dad walked in, just as she was

taking the first bite.

"Hi, Dad!" she called casually, careful not to meet his eye. "How was your day?"

Dad leant over to kiss her, and stroked her hair affectionately. Not wanting to worry his daughter, he was equally casual.

"Oh, you know," he said, "pretty routine. How about yours?"

Shirley hid a smile and shrugged nonchalantly.

"The same," she said, taking another bite. That was that, then! No need whatsoever for Dad to hear what she'd *really* been up to – the same way he had no intention of telling her!

She offered the tortilla up to her father. "Want some?"

"I… er… already ate," he said. The snacks that girl came up with sometimes were quite unbelievable and, to his mind, totally inedible!

Shirley sat down at the kitchen table to finish her tortilla, then took out her journal to write up the events of the fully-solved case. There was a lot to catch up on.

What a day! Bomb detonation, alien-catching, and pretend hypnosis... I can't quite believe I've just told Dad it was a 'routine' day! Still, speaking of routines, Mr Howie will be back in class tomorrow, no doubt still insisting that there's a rational explanation for everything. That's one good thing to come out of this whole story, I suppose... hopefully he'll be able to sleep better at night now Doctor Stavko has been found guilty of patient manipulation!

She was about to close the journal, then decided to add an extra thought:

In a way, I'm disappointed that real ETs weren't involved. I know something did happen to Alan Brooks two years ago. Something nobody can explain...

Shirley sighed, and then scribbled a final line:

But as we well know, when you've ruled out whatever is impossible, what remains – however unlikely – must be the truth.

It wasn't until she was walking upstairs past Gran's room that something caught her eye. She'd spent many hours looking at Gran's ancient artefacts, listening raptly to

Gran's stories about where they'd all come from, but tonight she noticed a small glass jar on the knick-knack shelf. She wondered why she'd never spotted it before.

She walked into the room without disturbing her grandmother, who was lost in one of her big archaeology books, and went over to the shelf to examine the jar more closely.

Inside it she saw... three tiny metal balls. Sort of ball-bearing size. Sort of... in-Mr-Howie's-neck size.

Shirley stared at the metal balls for a second and then looked over at Gran. She stole up behind her, still holding the jar, and took a closer look. Then she blinked and looked again.

There, on the nape of her grandmother's neck, was a small scar left by an incision of some kind.

Shirley stood frozen to the spot for a second. Did this mean that…

She shook her head. Unthinkable! Absolutely not!

But then she remembered the last words she'd just written in her journal:

…when you've ruled out whatever is impossible, what remains – however unlikely – must be the truth.

Back in her attic, Shirley added a final line to her journal.

I've come to the conclusion that sometimes truth really is stranger than fiction – especially in this house!

Who is Shirley Holmes?

THE ESSENTIAL CASE FILE
is the official guide to the exciting
action-adventure TV series.

Inside you will find:
- character profiles
- episode guides
- an introduction to some famous detectives
- amazing detective and crime-solving facts

plus hints, tips and exercises for you to
hone your own powers of observation,
deduction, perception, memory and
imagination!

FROM THE ACTION-ADVENTURE TV SERIES

THE ADVENTURES OF Shirley HOLMES

- ARSON ATTACKS ALL OVER TOWN...
- A NEW KID IN SCHOOL...
- A STICKY SITUATION...
- IS IT ALL TOO HOT TO HANDLE?

Shirley Holmes investigates in:

THE CASE OF THE BURNING BUILDING

Some of Shirley's schoolmates find her odd – Bo Sawchuk, the new kid, certainly does. But when he is accused of starting several fires in the area, proving his innocence becomes more important than avoiding the class weirdo.

Shirley is soon on the case, but realises she will have to convince Bo that the one person he trusts is not as honest as he seems. Her search for the truth puts her in great danger. Only Bo can save her – but will he?

FROM THE ACTION-ADVENTURE TV SERIES

- A HORSE BEHAVING STRANGELY...
- A FRIEND BEHAVING SECRETIVELY...
- A WEB OF LIES AND DECEIT...
  - IS THERE A COVER-UP AT THE RACECOURSE?

Shirley Holmes investigates in:

THE CASE OF THE BLAZING STAR

Anything out of the ordinary sets Shirley's brain cells tingling. When Bo Sawchuk begins behaving suspiciously, she doesn't think twice about making him the subject of her latest investigation – even though he's her best friend!

What Shirley uncovers is Bo's involvement with a local racing stable and a plan to make big money. Is her friend being forced back into a life of dishonesty? And, if he is, what will she do about it?

FROM THE ACTION-ADVENTURE TV SERIES

- RABBITS AND REPTILES ALL OVER THE PLACE ..
- A CLUE IN A VEGGIE BURGER...
- KIDNAPPING BY NUMBERS...
- IS THERE MADMAN ON THE LOOSE?

Shirley Holmes investigates in:

THE CASE OF THE DISAPPEARING DRAGON

A break-in at the local pet shop is just the first of a number of strange thefts. Animals are disappearing all over town – some are exotic and expensive, some are household pets and some are so rare they shouldn't even be available to steal!

Shirley is determined to track down the thieves and early clues lead her to suspect the work of the Animal Liberation Front. But, whoever is responsible, just where are they keeping all those animals?

FROM THE ACTION-ADVENTURE TV SERIES

Order Form

To order direct from the publishers, just make a list of the titles you want and fill in the form below:

Name

....

Address

....

....

....

Send to: Dept 6, HarperCollins Publishers Ltd, Westerhill Road, Bishopbriggs, Glasgow G64 2QT.

Please enclose a cheque or postal order to the value of the cover price, plus:

UK & BFPO: Add £1.00 for the first book, and 25p per copy for each additional book ordered.

Overseas and Eire: Add £2.95 service charge. Books will be sent by surface mail but quotes for airmail despatch will be given on request.

A 24-hour telephone ordering service is available to holders of Visa, MasterCard, Amex or Switch cards on 0141-772 2281.

Collins
An *Imprint* of HarperCollins*Publishers*